THE PROPHET

KHALIL GIBRAN

THE PROPHET

W. Books

This is a W. Books publication, a division of Grupo Ciranda Cultural.

Text: Lucy Maud Montgomery
First Publication: 1923
Graphic Design: Linea Editora
Cover: Ana Dobón

Dados Internacionais de Catalogação na Publicação (CIP) de acordo com ISBD

G447t Gibran, Kahlil.

The prophet / Kahlil Gibran. - Jandira, SP : W. Books, 2025.
64 p. : 12,80cm x 19,70cm. - (Classics).

ISBN: 978-65-83398-34-5

1. Literatura libanesa. 2. Romance. 3. Ação. 4. Aventura. 5. Ficção. I. Título. II. Série.

2024-2320 CDD 892.7
CDU 821.411.21

Elaborada por Lucio Feitosa - CRB-8/8803

Índice para catálogo sistemático:
1. Literatura libanesa 892.7
2. Literatura libanesa 821.411.21

www.cirandacultural.com.br

CONTENTS

THE COMING OF THE SHIP

Almustafa, the chosen and the beloved, who was a dawn unto his own day, had waited twelve years in the city of Orphalese for his ship that was to return and bear him back to the isle of his birth.

And in the twelfth year, on the seventh day of Ielool, the month of reaping, he climbed the hill without the city walls and looked seaward; and he beheld his ship coming with the mist.

Then the gates of his heart were flung open, and his joy flew far over the sea. And he closed his eyes and prayed in the silences of his soul.

But as he descended the hill, a sadness came upon him, and he thought in his heart:

How shall I go in peace and without sorrow? Nay, not without a wound in the spirit shall I leave this city. Long were the days of pain I have spent within its walls, and long were the nights of aloneness; and who can depart from his pain and his aloneness without regret?

Too many fragments of the spirit have I scattered in these streets, and too many are the children of my longing that walk naked among these hills, and I cannot withdraw from them without a burden and an ache.

It is not a garment I cast off this day, but a skin that I tear with my own hands.

Nor is it a thought I leave behind me, but a heart made sweet with hunger and with thirst.

Yet I cannot tarry longer.

The sea that calls all things unto her calls me, and I must embark.

For to stay, though the hours burn in the night, is to freeze and crystallize and be bound in a mould.

Fain would I take with me all that is here. But how shall I?

A voice cannot carry the tongue and the lips that gave it wings. Alone must it seek the ether.

And alone and without his nest shall the eagle fly across the sun.

Now when he reached the foot of the hill, he turned again towards the sea, and he saw his ship approaching the harbour, and upon her prow the mariners, the men of his own land.

And his soul cried out to them, and he said:

Sons of my ancient mother, you riders of the tides,

How often have you sailed in my dreams. And now you come in my awakening, which is my deeper dream.

Ready am I to go, and my eagerness with sails full set awaits the wind.

Only another breath will I breathe in this still air, only another loving look cast backward,

And then I shall stand among you, a seafarer among seafarers. And you, vast sea, sleepless mother,

Who alone are peace and freedom to the river and the stream,

Only another winding will this stream make, only another murmur in this glade,

And then shall I come to you, a boundless drop to a boundless ocean.

And as he walked he saw from afar men and women leaving their fields and their vineyards and hastening towards the city gates.

And he heard their voices calling his name, and shouting from field to field telling one another of the coming of his ship.

And he said to himself:

Shall the day of parting be the day of gathering?

And shall it be said that my eve was in truth my dawn?

And what shall I give unto him who has left his plough in mid-furrow, or to him who has stopped the wheel of his winepress? Shall my heart become a tree heavy-laden with fruit that I may gather and give unto them?

And shall my desires flow like a fountain that I may fill their cups?

Am I a harp that the hand of the mighty may touch me, or a flute that his breath may pass through me?

A seeker of silences am I, and what treasure have I found in silences that I may dispense with confidence?

If this is my day of harvest, in what fields have I sowed the seed, and in what unremembered seasons?

If this indeed be the hour in which I lift up my lantern, it is not my flame that shall burn therein.

Empty and dark shall I raise my lantern,

And the guardian of the night shall fill it with oil and he shall light it also.

These things he said in words. But much in his heart remained unsaid. For he himself could not speak his deeper secret.

And when he entered into the city all the people came to meet him, and they were crying out to him as with one voice.

And the elders of the city stood forth and said:

Go not yet away from us.

A noontide have you been in our twilight, and your youth has given us dreams to dream.

No stranger are you among us, nor a guest, but our son and our dearly beloved.

Suffer not yet our eyes to hunger for your face.

And the priests and the priestesses said unto him:

Let not the waves of the sea separate us now, and the years you have spent in our midst become a memory.

You have walked among us a spirit, and your shadow has been a light upon our faces.

Much have we loved you. But speechless was our love, and with veils has it been veiled.

Yet now it cries aloud unto you, and would stand revealed before you.

And ever has it been that love knows not its own depth until the hour of separation.

And others came also and entreated him. But he answered them not. He only bent his head; and those who stood near saw his tears falling upon his breast.

And he and the people proceeded towards the great square before the temple.

And there came out of the sanctuary a woman whose name was Almitra. And she was a seeress.

And he looked upon her with exceeding tenderness, for it was she who had first sought and believed in him when he had been but a day in their city. And she hailed him, saying:

Prophet of God, in quest of the uttermost, long have you searched the distances for your ship.

And now your ship has come, and you must needs go.

Deep is your longing for the land of your memories and the dwelling place of your greater desires; and our love would not bind you nor our needs hold you.

Yet this we ask ere you leave us, that you speak to us and give us of your truth.

And we will give it unto our children, and they unto their children, and it shall not perish.

In your aloneness you have watched with our days, and in your wakefulness you have listened to the weeping and the laughter of our sleep.

Now therefore disclose us to ourselves, and tell us all that has been shown you of that which is between birth and death.

And he answered,

People of Orphalese, of what can I speak save of that which is even now moving within your souls?

ON LOVE

Then said Almitra, Speak to us of ***Love***.

And he raised his head and looked upon the people, and there fell a stillness upon them. And with a great voice he said:

When love beckons to you, follow him,

Though his ways are hard and steep.

And when his wings enfold you yield to him,

Though the sword hidden among his pinions may wound you.

And when he speaks to you believe in him,

Though his voice may shatter your dreams as the north wind lays waste the garden.

For even as love crowns you so shall he crucify you. Even as he is for your growth so is he for your pruning.

Even as he ascends to your height and caresses your tenderest branches that quiver in the sun,

So shall he descend to your roots and shake them in their clinging to the earth.

Like sheaves of corn he gathers you unto himself.

He threshes you to make you naked.

He sifts you to free you from your husks.

He grinds you to whiteness.

He kneads you until you are pliant;

And then he assigns you to his sacred fire, that you may become sacred bread for God's sacred feast.

All these things shall love do unto you that you may know the secrets of your heart, and in that knowledge become a fragment of Life's heart.

But if in your fear you would seek only love's peace and love's pleasure,

Then it is better for you that you cover your nakedness and pass out of love's threshing-floor,

Into the seasonless world where you shall laugh, but not all of your laughter, and weep, but not all of your tears.

Love gives naught but itself and takes naught but from itself.

Love possesses not nor would it be possessed;

For love is sufficient unto love.

When you love you should not say, "God is in my heart," but rather, "I am in the heart of God."

And think not you can direct the course of love, for love, if it finds you worthy, directs your course.

Love has no other desire but to fulfil itself.

But if you love and must needs have desires, let these be your desires:

To melt and be like a running brook that sings its melody to the night. To know the pain of too much tenderness.

To be wounded by your own understanding of love;

And to bleed willingly and joyfully.

To wake at dawn with a winged heart and give thanks for another day of loving;

To rest at the noon hour and meditate love's ecstacy;

To return home at eventide with gratitude;

And then to sleep with a prayer for the beloved in your heart and a song of praise upon your lips.

ON MARRIAGE

Then Almitra spoke again and said, And what of ***Marriage*** master?

And he answered saying:

You were born together, and together you shall be forevermore.

You shall be together when the white wings of death scatter your days.

Aye, you shall be together even in the silent memory of God.

But let there be spaces in your togetherness,

And let the winds of the heavens dance between you.

Love one another, but make not a bond of love:

Let it rather be a moving sea between the shores of your souls.

Fill each other's cup but drink not from one cup.

Give one another of your bread but eat not from the same loaf. Sing and dance together and be joyous, but let each one of you be alone,

Even as the strings of a lute are alone though they quiver with the same music.

Give your hearts, but not into each other's keeping.

For only the hand of Life can contain your hearts.

And stand together yet not too near together:

For the pillars of the temple stand apart, And the oak tree and the cypress grow not in each other's shadow.

ON CHILDREN

And a woman who held a babe against her bosom said, Speak to us of ***Children***.

And he said:

Your children are not your children.

They are the sons and daughters of Life's longing for itself.

They come through you but not from you,

And though they are with you yet they belong not to you.

You may give them your love but not your thoughts,

For they have their own thoughts.

You may house their bodies but not their souls,

For their souls dwell in the house of tomorrow, which you cannot visit, not even in your dreams.

You may strive to be like them, but seek not to make them like you. For life goes not backward nor tarries with yesterday.

You are the bows from which your children as living arrows are sent forth.

The archer sees the mark upon the path of the infinite, and He bends you with His might that His arrows may go swift and far.

Let your bending in the Archer's hand be for gladness;

For even as he loves the arrow that flies, so He loves also the bow that is stable.

ON GIVING

Then said a rich man, Speak to us of ***Giving***.

And he answered:

You give but little when you give of your possessions.

It is when you give of yourself that you truly give.

For what are your possessions but things you keep and guard for fear you may need them tomorrow?

And tomorrow, what shall tomorrow bring to the overprudent dog burying bones in the trackless sand as he follows the pilgrims to the holy city?

And what is fear of need but need itself?

Is not dread of thirst when your well is full, the thirst that is unquenchable?

There are those who give little of the much which they have—and they give it for recognition and their hidden desire makes their gifts unwholesome.

And there are those who have little and give it all.

These are the believers in life and the bounty of life, and their coffer is never empty.

There are those who give with joy, and that joy is their reward.

And there are those who give with pain, and that pain is their baptism.

And there are those who give and know not pain in giving, nor do they seek joy, nor give with mindfulness of virtue;

They give as in yonder valley the myrtle breathes its fragrance into space.

Through the hands of such as these God speaks, and from behind their eyes He smiles upon the earth.

It is well to give when asked, but it is better to give unasked, through understanding;

And to the open-handed the search for one who shall receive is joy greater than giving.

And is there aught you would withhold?

All you have shall some day be given;

Therefore give now, that the season of giving may be yours and not your inheritors'.

You often say, "I would give, but only to the deserving."

The trees in your orchard say not so, nor the flocks in your pasture.

They give that they may live, for to withhold is to perish.

Surely he who is worthy to receive his days and his nights, is worthy of all else from you.

And he who has deserved to drink from the ocean of life deserves to fill his cup from your little stream.

And what desert greater shall there be, than that which lies in the courage and the confidence, nay the charity, of receiving?

And who are you that men should rend their bosom and unveil their pride, that you may see their worth naked and their pride unabashed?

See first that you yourself deserve to be a giver, and an instrument of giving.

For in truth it is life that gives unto life—while you, who deem yourself a giver, are but a witness.

And you receivers—and you are all receivers—assume no weight of gratitude, lest you lay a yoke upon yourself and upon him who gives.

Rather rise together with the giver on his gifts as on wings;

For to be overmindful of your debt, is ito doubt his generosity who has the freehearted earth for mother, and God for father.

ON EATING AND DRINKING

Then an old man, a keeper of an inn, said, Speak to us of ***Eating and Drinking***.

And he said:

Would that you could live on the fragrance of the earth, and like an air plant be sustained by the light.

But since you must kill to eat, and rob the newly born of its mother's milk to quench your thirst, let it then be an act of worship,

And let your board stand an altar on which the pure and the innocent of forest and plain are sacrificed for that which is purer and still more innocent in man.

When you kill a beast say to him in your heart,

"By the same power that slays you, I too am slain; and I too shall be consumed. For the law that delivered you into my hand shall deliver me into a mightier hand.

Your blood and my blood is naught but the sap that feeds the tree of heaven."

And when you crush an apple with your teeth, say to it in your heart,

"Your seeds shall live in my body,

And the buds of your tomorrow shall blossom in my heart,

And your fragrance shall be my breath, And together we shall rejoice through all the seasons."

And in the autumn, when you gather the grapes of your vineyards for the winepress, say in your heart,

"I too am a vineyard, and my fruit shall be gathered for the winepress,

And like new wine I shall be kept in eternal vessels."

And in winter, when you draw the wine, let there be in your heart a song for each cup;

And let there be in the song a remembrance for the autumn days, and for the vineyard, and for the winepress.

ON WORK

Then a ploughman said, Speak to us of ***Work***.

And he answered, saying:

You work that you may keep pace with the earth and the soul of the earth.

For to be idle is to become a stranger unto the seasons, and to step out of life's procession, that marches in majesty and proud submission towards the infinite.

When you work you are a flute through whose heart the whispering of the hours turns to music.

Which of you would be a reed, dumb and silent, when all else sings together in unison?

Always you have been told that work is a curse and labour a misfortune.

But I say to you that when you work you fulfil a part of earth's furthest dream, assigned to you when that dream was born,

And in keeping yourself with labour you are in truth loving life,

And to love life through labour is to be intimate with life's inmost secret.

But if you in your pain call birth an affliction and the support of the flesh a curse written upon your brow, then I answer that naught but the sweat of your brow shall wash away that which is written.

You have been told also that life is darkness, and in your weariness you echo what was said by the weary.

And I say that life is indeed darkness 'save when there is urge,

And all urge is blind save when there is knowledge,

And all knowledge is vain save when there is work,

And all work is empty save when there is love;

And when you work with love you bind yourself to yourself, and to one another, and to God.

And what is it to work with love?

It is to weave the cloth with threads drawn from your heart, even as if your beloved were to wear that cloth.

It is to build a house with affection, even as if your beloved were to dwell in that house.

It is to sow seeds with tenderness and reap the harvest with joy, even as if your beloved were to eat the fruit.

It is to charge all things you fashion with a breath of your own spirit,

And to know that all the blessed dead are standing about you and watching.

Often have I heard you say, as if speaking in sleep, "He who works in marble, and finds the shape of his own soul in the stone, is nobler than he who ploughs the soil. And he who seizes the rainbow to lay it on a cloth in the likeness of man, is more than he who makes the sandals for our feet."

But I say, not in sleep but in the overwakefulness of noontide, that the wind speaks not more sweetly to the giant oaks than to the least of all the blades of grass;

And he alone is great who turns the voice of the wind into a song made sweeter by his own loving.

Work is love made visible.

And if you cannot work with love but only with distaste, it is better that you should leave your work and sit at the gate of the temple and take alms of those who work with joy.

For if you bake bread with indifference, you bake a bitter bread that feeds but half man's hunger.

And if you grudge the crushing of the grapes, your grudge distils a poison in the wine. And if you sing though as angels, and love not the singing, you muffle man's ears to the voices of the day and the voices of the night.

ON JOY AND SORROW

Then a woman said, Speak to us of ***Joy and Sorrow***.

And he answered:

Your joy is your sorrow unmasked.

And the selfsame well from which your laughter rises was oftentimes filled with your tears.

And how else can it be?

The deeper that sorrow carves into your being, the more joy you can contain.

Is not the cup that holds your wine the very cup that was burned in the potter's oven?

And is not the lute that soothes your spirit, the very wood that was hollowed with knives?

When you are joyous, look deep into your heart and you shall find it is only that which has given you sorrow that is giving you joy.

When you are sorrowful look again in your heart, and you shall see that in truth you are weeping for that which has been your delight.

Some of you say, "Joy is greater than sorrow," and others say, "Nay, sorrow is the greater."

But I say unto you, they are inseparable.

Together they come, and when one sits alone with you at your board, remember that the other is asleep upon your bed.

Verily you are suspended like scales between your sorrow and your joy.

Only when you are empty are you at standstill and balanced.

When the treasure-keeper lifts you to weigh his gold and his silver, needs must your joy or your sorrow rise or fall.

ON HOUSES

Then a mason came forth and said, Speak to us of ***Houses***.

And he answered and said:

Build of your imaginings a bower in the wilderness ere you build a house within the city walls.

For even as you have home-comings in your twilight, so has the wanderer in you, the ever distant and alone.

Your house is your larger body.

It grows in the sun and sleeps in the stillness of the night; and it is not dreamless. Does not your house dream? and dreaming, leave the city for grove or hilltop?

Would that I could gather your houses into my hand, and like a sower scatter them in forest and meadow.

Would the valleys were your streets, and the green paths your alleys, that you might seek one another through vineyards, and come with the fragrance of the earth in your garments.

But these things are not yet to be.

In their fear your forefathers gathered you too near together. And that fear shall endure a little longer. A little longer shall your city walls separate your hearths from your fields.

And tell me, people of Orphalese, what have you in these houses? And what is it you guard with fastened doors?

Have you peace, the quiet urge that reveals your power?

Have you remembrances, the glimmering arches that span the summits of the mind?

Have you beauty, that leads the heart from things fashioned of wood and stone to the holy mountain?

Tell me, have you these in your houses?

Or have you only comfort, and the lust for comfort, that stealthy thing that enters the house a guest, and then becomes a host, and then a master?

Ay, and it becomes a tamer, and with hook and scourge makes puppets of your larger desires.

Though its hands are silken, its heart is of iron.

It lulls you to sleep only to stand by your bed and jeer at the dignity of the flesh.

It makes mock of your sound senses, and lays them in thistle-down like fragile vessels.

Verily the lust for comfort murders the passion of the soul, and then walks grinning in the funeral.

But you, children of space, you restless in rest, you shall not be trapped nor tamed.

Your house shall be not an anchor but a mast.

It shall not be a glistening film that covers a wound, but an eyelid that guards the eye.

You shall not fold your wings that you may pass through doors, nor bend your heads that they strike not against a ceiling, nor fear to breathe lest walls should crack and fall down.

You shall not dwell in tombs made by the dead for the living.

And though of magnificence and splendour, your house shall not hold your secret nor shelter your longing.

For that which is boundless in you abides in the mansion of the sky, whose door is the morning mist, and whose windows are the songs and the silences of night.

ON CLOTHES

And the weaver said, Speak to us of ***Clothes***.

And he answered:

Your clothes conceal much of your beauty, yet they hide not the unbeautiful.

And though you seek in garments the freedom of privacy you may find in them a harness and a chain.

Would that you could meet the sun and the wind with more of your skin and less of your raiment,

For the breath of life is in the sunlight and the hand of life is in the wind.

Some of you say, "It is the north wind who has woven the clothes we wear."

And I say, Ay, it was the north wind,

But shame was his loom, and the softening of the sinews was his thread.

And when his work was done he laughed in the forest. Forget not that modesty is for a shield against the eye of the unclean.

And when the unclean shall be no more, what were modesty but a fetter and a fouling of the mind?

And forget not that the earth delights to feel your bare feet and the winds long to play with your hair.

ON BUYING AND SELLING

And a merchant said, Speak to us of ***Buying and Selling***.

And he answered and said:

To you the earth yields her fruit, and you shall not want if you but know how to fill your hands.

It is in exchanging the gifts of the earth that you shall find abundance and be satisfied.

Yet unless the exchange be in love and kindly justice, it will but lead some to greed and others to hunger.

When in the market place you toilers of the sea and fields and vineyards meet the weavers and the potters and the gatherers of spices,—

Invoke then the master spirit of the earth, to come into your midst and sanctify the scales and the reckoning that weighs value against value. And suffer not the barren-handed to take part in your transactions, who would sell their words for your labour.

To such men you should say,

"Come with us to the field, or go with our brothers to the sea and cast your net;

For the land and the sea shall be bountiful to you even as to us."

And if there come the singers and the dancers and the flute players,—buy of their gifts also.

For they too are gatherers of fruit and frankincense, and that which they bring, though fashioned of dreams, is raiment and food for your soul.

And before you leave the market place, see that no one has gone his way with empty hands.

For the master spirit of the earth shall not sleep peacefully upon the wind till the needs of the least of you are satisfied.

ON CRIME AND PUNISHMENT

Then one of the judges of the city stood forth and said, Speak to us of ***Crime and Punishment***.

And he answered, saying:

It is when your spirit goes wandering upon the wind,

That you, alone and unguarded, commit a wrong unto others and therefore unto yourself.

And for that wrong committed must you knock and wait a while unheeded at the gate of the blessed.

Like the ocean is your god-self;

It remains for ever undefiled.

And like the ether it lifts but the winged.

Even like the sun is your god-self;

It knows not the ways of the mole nor seeks it the holes of the serpent. But your god-self dwells not alone in your being.

Much in you is still man, and much in you is not yet man,

But a shapeless pigmy that walks asleep in the mist searching for its own awakening.

And of the man in you would I now speak.

For it is he and not your god-self nor the pigmy in the mist, that knows crime and the punishment of crime.

Oftentimes have I heard you speak of one who commits a wrong as though he were not one of you, but a stranger unto you and an intruder upon your world.

But I say that even as the holy and the righteous cannot rise beyond the highest which is in each one of you,

So the wicked and the weak cannot fall lower than the lowest which is in you also.

And as a single leaf turns not yellow but with the silent knowledge of the whole tree, So the wrong-doer cannot do wrong without the hidden will of you all.

Like a procession you walk together towards your god-self.

You are the way and the wayfarers.

And when one of you falls down he falls for those behind him, a caution against the stumbling stone.

Ay, and he falls for those ahead of him, who though faster and surer of foot, yet removed not the stumbling stone.

And this also, though the word lie heavy upon your hearts:

The murdered is not unaccountable for his own murder,

And the robbed is not blameless in being robbed.

The righteous is not innocent of the deeds of the wicked,

And the white-handed is not clean in the doings of the felon.

Yea, the guilty is oftentimes the victim of the injured,

And still more often the condemned is the burden bearer for the guiltless and unblamed.

You cannot separate the just from the unjust and the good from the wicked;

For they stand together before the face of the sun even as the black thread and the white are woven together.

And when the black thread breaks, the weaver shall look into the whole cloth, and he shall examine the loom also.

If any of you would bring to judgment the unfaithful wife,

Let him also weigh the heart of her husband in scales, and measure his soul with measurements.

And let him who would lash the offender look unto the spirit of the offended.

And if any of you would punish in the name of righteousness and lay the ax unto the evil tree, let him see to its roots;

And verily he will find the roots of the good and the bad, the fruitful and the fruitless, all entwined together in the silent heart of the earth.

And you judges who would be just,

What judgment pronounce you upon him who though honest in the flesh yet is a thief in spirit?

What penalty lay you upon him who slays in the flesh yet is himself slain in the spirit?

And how prosecute you him who in action is a deceiver and an oppressor,

Yet who also is aggrieved and outraged?

And how shall you punish those whose remorse is already greater than their misdeeds?

Is not remorse the justice which is administered by that very law which you would fain serve?

Yet you cannot lay remorse upon the innocent nor lift it from the heart of the guilty.

Unbidden shall it call in the night, that men may wake and gaze upon themselves. And you who would understand justice, how shall you unless you look upon all deeds in the fullness of light?

Only then shall you know that the erect and the fallen are but one man standing in twilight between the night of his pigmy-self and the day of his god-self, And that the corner-stone of the temple is not higher than the lowest stone in its foundation.

ON LAWS

Then a lawyer said, But what of our ***Laws***, master?

And he answered:

You delight in laying down laws,

Yet you delight more in breaking them.

Like children playing by the ocean who build sand-towers with constancy and then destroy them with laughter.

But while you build your sand-towers the ocean brings more sand to the shore,

And when you destroy them the ocean laughs with you.

Verily the ocean laughs always with the innocent.

But what of those to whom life is not an ocean, and man-made laws are not sand-towers,

But to whom life is a rock, and the law a chisel with which they would carve it in their own likeness? What of the cripple who hates dancers?

What of the ox who loves his yoke and deems the elk and deer of the forest stray and vagrant things?

What of the old serpent who cannot shed his skin, and calls all others naked and shameless?

And of him who comes early to the wedding-feast, and when over-fed and tired goes his way saying that all feasts are violation and all feasters lawbreakers?

What shall I say of these save that they too stand in the sunlight, but with their backs to the sun?

They see only their shadows, and their shadows are their laws.

And what is the sun to them but a caster of shadows?

And what is it to acknowledge the laws but to stoop down and trace their shadows upon the earth?

But you who walk facing the sun, what images drawn on the earth can hold you?

You who travel with the wind, what weather-vane shall direct your course?

What man's law shall bind you if you break your yoke but upon no man's prison door?

What laws shall you fear if you dance but stumble against no man's iron chains?

And who is he that shall bring you to judgment if you tear off your garment yet leave it in no man's path?

People of Orphalese, you can muffle the drum, and you can loosen the strings of the lyre, but who shall command the skylark not to sing?

ON FREEDOM

And an orator said, Speak to us of ***Freedom***.

And he answered:

At the city gate and by your fireside I have seen you prostrate yourself and worship your own freedom,

Even as slaves humble themselves before a tyrant and praise him though he slays them.

Ay, in the grove of the temple and in the shadow of the citadel I have seen the freest among you wear their freedom as a yoke and a handcuff.

And my heart bled within me; for you can only be free when even the desire of seeking freedom becomes a harness to you, and when you cease to speak of freedom as a goal and a fulfilment.

You shall be free indeed when your days are not without a care nor your nights without a want and a grief,

But rather when these things girdle your life and yet you rise above them naked and unbound.

And how shall you rise beyond your days and nights unless you break the chains which you at the dawn of your understanding have fastened around your noon hour?

In truth that which you call freedom is the strongest of these chains, though its links glitter in the sun and dazzle your eyes.

And what is it but fragments of your own self you would discard that you may become free?

If it is an unjust law you would abolish, that law was written with your own hand upon your own forehead.

You cannot erase it by burning your law books nor by washing the foreheads of your judges, though you pour the sea upon them.

And if it is a despot you would dethrone, see first that his throne erected within you is destroyed.

For how can a tyrant rule the free and the proud, but for a tyranny in their own freedom and a shame in their own pride?

And if it is a care you would cast off, that cart has been chosen by you rather than imposed upon you.

And if it is a fear you would dispel, the seat of that fear is in your heart and not in the hand of the feared.

Verily all things move within your being in constant half embrace, the desired and the dreaded, the repugnant and the cherished, the pursued and that which you would escape.

These things move within you as lights and shadows in pairs that cling.

And when the shadow fades and is no more, the light that lingers becomes a shadow to another light.

And thus your freedom when it loses its fetters becomes itself the fetter of a greater freedom.

ON REASON AND PASSION

And the priestess spoke again and said: Speak to us of ***Reason and Passion***.

And he answered, saying:

Your soul is oftentimes a battlefield, upon which your reason and your judgment wage war against your passion and your appetite.

Would that I could be the peacemaker in your soul, that I might turn the discord and the rivalry of your elements into oneness and melody.

But how shall I, unless you yourselves be also the peacemakers, nay, the lovers of all your elements?

Your reason and your passion are the rudder and the sails of your seafaring soul.

If either your sails or your rudder be broken, you can but toss and drift, or else be held at a standstill in mid-seas. For reason, ruling alone, is a force confining; and passion, unattended, is a flame that burns to its own destruction.

Therefore let your soul exalt your reason to the height of passion, that it may sing;

And let it direct your passion with reason, that your passion may live through its own daily resurrection, and like the phoenix rise above its own ashes.

I would have you consider your judgment and your appetite even as you would two loved guests in your house.

Surely you would not honour one guest above the other; for he who is more mindful of one loses the love and the faith of both

Among the hills, when you sit in the cool shade of the white poplars, sharing the peace and serenity of distant fields and meadows—then let your heart say in silence, "God rests in reason."

And when the storm comes, and the mighty wind shakes the forest, and thunder and lightning proclaim the majesty of the sky,—then let your heart say in awe, "God moves in passion."

And since you are a breath in God's sphere, and a leaf in God's forest, you too should rest in reason and move in passion.

ON PAIN

And a woman spoke, saying, Tell us of ***Pain***.

And he said:

Your pain is the breaking of the shell that encloses your understanding.

Even as the stone of the fruit must break, that its heart may stand in the sun, so must you know pain.

And could you keep your heart in wonder at the daily miracles of your life, your pain would not seem less wondrous than your joy;

And you would accept the seasons of your heart, even as you have always accepted the seasons that pass over your fields.

And you would watch with serenity through the winters of your grief.

Much of your pain is self-chosen.

It is the bitter potion by which the physician within you heals your sick self.

Therefore trust the physician, and drink his remedy in silence and tranquillity: For his hand, though heavy and hard, is guided by the tender hand of the Unseen, And the cup he brings, though it burn your lips, has been fashioned of the clay which the Potter has moistened with His own sacred tears.

ON SELF-KNOWLEDGE

And a man said, Speak to us of ***Self-Knowledge***.

And he answered, saying:

Your hearts know in silence the secrets of the days and the nights.

But your ears thirst for the sound of your heart's knowledge.

You would know in words that which you have always known in thought.

You would touch with your fingers the naked body of your dreams.

And it is well you should.

The hidden well-spring of your soul must needs rise and run murmuring to the sea;

And the treasure of your infinite depths would be revealed to your eyes.

But let there be no scales to weigh your unknown treasure;

And seek not the depths of your knowledge with staff or sounding line.

For self is a sea boundless and measureless.

Say not, "I have found the truth," but rather, "I have found a truth."

Say not, "I have found the path of the soul." Say rather, "I have met the soul walking upon my path."

For the soul walks upon all paths.

The soul walks not upon a line, neither does it grow like a reed.

The soul unfolds itself, like a lotus of countless petals.

ON TEACHING

Then said a teacher, Speak to us of ***Teaching***.

And he said:

"No man can reveal to you aught but that which already lies half asleep in the dawning of your knowledge.

The teacher who walks in the shadow of the temple, among his followers, gives not of his wisdom but rather of his faith and his lovingness.

If he is indeed wise he does not bid you enter the house of his wisdom, but rather leads you to the threshold of your own mind.

The astronomer may speak to you of his understanding of space, but he cannot give you his understanding.

The musician may sing to you of the rhythm which is in all space, but he cannot give you the ear which arrests the rhythm nor the voice that echoes it. And he who is versed in the science of numbers can tell of the regions of weight and measure, but he cannot conduct you thither.

For the vision of one man lends not its wings to another man.

And even as each one of you stands alone in God's knowledge, so must each one of you be alone in his knowledge of God and in his understanding of the earth.

ON FRIENDSHIP

And a youth said, Speak to us of ***Friendship***.

And he answered, saying:

Your friend is your needs answered.

He is your field which you sow with love and reap with thanksgiving.

And he is your board and your fireside.

For you come to him with your hunger, and you seek him for peace.

When your friend speaks his mind you fear not the "nay" in your own mind, nor do you withhold the "ay."

And when he is silent your heart ceases not to listen to his heart;

For without words, in friendship, all thoughts, all desires, all expectations are born and shared, with joy that is unacclaimed.

When you part from your friend, you grieve not;

For that which you love most in him may be clearer in his absence, as the mountain to the climber is clearer from the plain. And let there be no purpose in friendship save the deepening of the spirit.

For love that seeks aught but the disclosure of its own mystery is not love but a net cast forth: and only the unprofitable is caught.

And let your best be for your friend.

If he must know the ebb of your tide, let him know its flood also.

For what is your friend that you should seek him with hours to kill?

Seek him always with hours to live.

For it is his to fill your need, but not your emptiness.

And in the sweetness of friendship let there be laughter, and sharing of pleasures.

For in the dew of little things the heart finds its morning and is refreshed.

ON TALKING

And then a scholar said, Speak of ***Talking***.

And he answered, saying:

You talk when you cease to be at peace with your thoughts;

And when you can no longer dwell in the solitude of your heart you live in your lips, and sound is a diversion and a pastime.

And in much of your talking, thinking is half murdered.

For thought is a bird of space, that in a cage of words may indeed unfold its wings but cannot fly.

There are those among you who seek the talkative through fear of being alone.

The silence of aloneness reveals to their eyes their naked selves and they would escape.

And there are those who talk, and without knowledge or forethought reveal a truth which they themselves do not understand.

And there are those who have the truth within them, but they tell it not in words.

In the bosom of such as these the spirit dwells in rhythmic silence.

When you meet your friend on the roadside or in the market place, let the spirit in you move your lips and direct your tongue.

Let the voice within your voice speak to the ear of his ear;

For his soul will keep the truth of your heart as the taste of the wine is remembered

When the colour is forgotten and the vessel is no more.

ON TIME

And an astronomer said, Master, what of ***Time***?

And he answered:

You would measure time the measureless and the immeasurable.

You would adjust your conduct and even direct the course of your spirit according to hours and seasons.

Of time you would make a stream upon whose bank you would sit and watch its flowing.

Yet the timeless in you is aware of life's timelessness,

And knows that yesterday is but today's memory and tomorrow is today's dream.

And that that which sings and contemplates in you is still dwelling within the bounds of that first moment which scattered the stars into space. Who among you does not feel that his power to love is boundless?

And yet who does not feel that very love, though boundless, encompassed within the centre of his being, and moving not from love thought to love thought, nor from love deeds to other love deeds?

And is not time even as love is, undivided and paceless?

But if in your thought you must measure time into seasons, let each season encircle all the other seasons,

And let today embrace the past with remembrance and the future with longing.

ON GOOD AND EVIL

And one of the elders of the city said, Speak to us of ***Good and Evil***.

And he answered:

Of the good in you I can speak, but not of the evil.

For what is evil but good tortured by its own hunger and thirst?

Verily when good is hungry it seeks food even in dark caves, and when it thirsts it drinks even of dead waters.

You are good when you are one with yourself.

Yet when you are not one with yourself you are not evil.

For a divided house is not a den of thieves; it is only a divided house.

And a ship without rudder may wander aimlessly among perilous isles yet sink not to the bottom. You are good when you strive to give of yourself.

Yet you are not evil when you seek gain for yourself.

For when you strive for gain you are but a root that clings to the earth and sucks at her breast.

Surely the fruit cannot say to the root, "Be like me, ripe and full and ever giving of your abundance."

For to the fruit giving is a need, as receiving is a need to the root.

You are good when you are fully awake in your speech,

Yet you are not evil when you sleep while your tongue staggers without purpose.

And even stumbling speech may strengthen a weak tongue.

You are good when you walk to your goal firmly and with bold steps.

Yet you are not evil when you go thither limping. Even those who limp go not backward.

But you who are strong and swift, see that you do not limp before the lame, deeming it kindness.

You are good in countless ways, and you are not evil when you are not good,

You are only loitering and sluggard.

Pity that the stags cannot teach swiftness to the turtles.

In your longing for your giant self lies your goodness: and that longing is in all of you.

But in some of you that longing is a torrent rushing with might to the sea, carrying the secrets of the hillsides and the songs of the forest.

And in others it is a flat stream that loses itself in angles and bends and lingers before it reaches the shore.

But let not him who longs much say to him who longs little, "Wherefore are you slow and halting?"

For the truly good ask not the naked, "Where is your garment?" nor the houseless, "What has befallen your house?"

ON PRAYER

Then a priestess said, Speak to us of ***Prayer***.

And he answered, saying:

You pray in your distress and in your need; would that you might pray also in the fullness of your joy and in your days of abundance.

For what is prayer but the expansion of yourself into the living ether?

And if it is for your comfort to pour your darkness into space, it is also for your delight to pour forth the dawning of your heart.

And if you cannot but weep when your soul summons you to prayer, she should spur you again and yet again, though weeping, until you shall come laughing.

When you pray you rise to meet in the air those who are praying at that very hour, and whom save in prayer you may not meet.

Therefore let your visit to that temple invisible be for naught but ecstasy and sweet communion.

For if you should enter the temple for no other purpose than asking you shall not receive:

And if you should enter into it to humble yourself you shall not be lifted:

Or even if you should enter into it to beg for the good of others you shall not be heard.

It is enough that you enter the temple invisible.

I cannot teach you how to pray in words.

God listens not to your words save when He Himself utters them through your lips.

And I cannot teach you the prayer of the seas and the forests and the mountains. But you who are born of the mountains and the forests and the seas can find their prayer in your heart,

And if you but listen in the stillness of the night you shall hear them saying in silence,

"Our God, who art our winged self, it is thy will in us that willeth.

It is thy desire in us that desireth.

It is thy urge in us that would turn our nights, which are thine, into days which are thine also.

We cannot ask thee for aught, for thou knowest our needs before they are born in us:

Thou art our need; and in giving us more of thyself thou givest us all."

ON PLEASURE

Then a hermit, who visited the city once a year, came forth and said, Speak to us of ***Pleasure***.

And he answered, saying:

Pleasure is a freedom-song,

But it is not freedom.

It is the blossoming of your desires,

But it is not their fruit.

It is a depth calling unto a height,

But it is not the deep nor the high.

It is the caged taking wing,

But it is not space encompassed.

Ay, in very truth, pleasure is a freedom-song.

And I fain would have you sing it with fullness of heart; yet I would not have you lose your hearts in the singing.

Some of your youth seek pleasure as if it were all, and they are judged and rebuked. I would not judge nor rebuke them. I would have them seek.

For they shall find pleasure, but not her alone;

Seven are her sisters, and the least of them is more beautiful than pleasure.

Have you not heard of the man who was digging in the earth for roots and found a treasure?

And some of your elders remember pleasures with regret like wrongs committed in drunkenness.

But regret is the beclouding of the mind and not its chastisement.

They should remember their pleasures with gratitude, as they would the harvest of a summer.

Yet if it comforts them to regret, let them be comforted.

And there are among you those who are neither young to seek nor old to remember;

And in their fear of seeking and remembering they shun all pleasures, lest they neglect the spirit or offend against it.

But even in their foregoing is their pleasure.

And thus they too find a treasure though they dig for roots with quivering hands.

But tell me, who is he that can offend the spirit?

Shall the nightingale offend the stillness of the night, or the firefly the stars?

And shall your flame or your smoke burden the wind?

Think you the spirit is a still pool which you can trouble with a staff?

Oftentimes in denying yourself pleasure you do but store the desire in the recesses of your being.

Who knows but that which seems omitted today, waits for tomorrow?

Even your body knows its heritage and its rightful need and will not be deceived.

And your body is the harp of your soul,

And it is yours to bring forth sweet music from it or confused sounds.

And now you ask in your heart, "How shall we distinguish that which is good in pleasure from that which is not good?"

Go to your fields and your gardens, and you shall learn that it is the pleasure of the bee to gather honey of the flower,

But it is also the pleasure of the flower to yield its honey to the bee.

For to the bee a flower is a fountain of life,

And to the flower a bee is a messenger of love,

And to both, bee and flower, the giving and the receiving of pleasure is a need and an ecstasy.

People of Orphalese, be in your pleasures like the flowers and the bees.

ON BEAUTY

And a poet said, Speak to us of ***Beauty***.

And he answered:

Where shall you seek beauty, and how shall you find her unless she herself be your way and your guide?

And how shall you speak of her except she be the weaver of your speech?

The aggrieved and the injured say, "Beauty is kind and gentle.

Like a young mother half-shy of her own glory she walks among us."

And the passionate say, "Nay, beauty is a thing of might and dread.

Like the tempest she shakes the earth beneath us and the sky above us."

The tired and the weary say, "Beauty is of soft whisperings. She speaks in our spirit. Her voice yields to our silences like a faint light that quivers in fear of the shadow."

But the restless say, "We have heard her shouting among the mountains,

And with her cries came the sound of hoofs, and the beating of wings and the roaring of lions."

At night the watchmen of the city say, "Beauty shall rise with the dawn from the east."

And at noontide the toilers and the wayfarers say, "We have seen her leaning over the earth from the windows of the sunset."

In winter say the snow-bound, "She shall come with the spring leaping upon the hills."

And in the summer heat the reapers say, "We have seen her dancing with the autumn leaves, and we saw a drift of snow in her hair." All these things have you said of beauty,

Yet in truth you spoke not of her but of needs unsatisfied,

And beauty is not a need but an ecstasy.

It is not a mouth thirsting nor an empty hand stretched forth,

But rather a heart enflamed and a soul enchanted.

It is not the image you would see nor the song you would hear,

But rather an image you see though you close your eyes and a song you hear though you shut your ears.

It is not the sap within the furrowed bark, nor a wing attached to a claw,

But rather a garden for ever in bloom and a flock of angels for ever in flight.

People of Orphalese, beauty is life when life unveils her holy face.

But you are life and you are the veil. Beauty is eternity gazing at itself in a mirror.

But you are eternity and you are the mirror.

ON RELIGION

And an old priest said, Speak to us of ***Religion***.

And he said:

Have I spoken this day of aught else?

Is not religion all deeds and all reflection,

And that which is neither deed nor reflection, but a wonder and a surprise ever springing in the soul, even while the hands hew the stone or tend the loom?

Who can separate his faith from his actions, or his belief from his occupations?

Who can spread his hours before him, saying, "This for God and this for myself; This for my soul, and this other for my body?"

All your hours are wings that beat through space from self to self. He who wears his morality but as his best garment were better naked.

The wind and the sun will tear no holes in his skin.

And he who defines his conduct by ethics imprisons his song-bird in a cage.

The freest song comes not through bars and wires.

And he to whom worshipping is a window, to open but also to shut, has not yet visited the house of his soul whose windows are from dawn to dawn.

Your daily life is your temple and your religion.

Whenever you enter into it take with you your all.

Take the plough and the forge and the mallet and the lute,

The things you have fashioned in necessity or for delight.

For in revery you cannot rise above your achievements nor fall lower than your failures.

And take with you all men: For in adoration you cannot fly higher than their hopes nor humble yourself lower than their despair.

And if you would know God be not therefore a solver of riddles.

Rather look about you and you shall see Him playing with your children.

And look into space; you shall see Him walking in the cloud, outstretching His arms in the lightning and descending in rain.

You shall see Him smiling in flowers, then rising and waving His hands in trees.

ON DEATH

Then Almitra spoke, saying, We would ask now of ***Death***.

And he said:

You would know the secret of death.

But how shall you find it unless you seek it in the heart of life?

The owl whose night-bound eyes are blind unto the day cannot unveil the mystery of light.

If you would indeed behold the spirit of death, open your heart wide unto the body of life.

For life and death are one, even as the river and the sea are one.

In the depth of your hopes and desires lies your silent knowledge of the beyond;

And like seeds dreaming beneath the snow your heart dreams of spring.

Trust the dreams, for in them is hidden the gate to eternity. Your fear of death is but the trembling of the shepherd when he stands before the king whose hand is to be laid upon him in honour.

Is the shepherd not joyful beneath his trembling, that he shall wear the mark of the king?

Yet is he not more mindful of his trembling?

For what is it to die but to stand naked in the wind and to melt into the sun?

And what is it to cease breathing, but to free the breath from its restless tides, that it may rise and expand and seek God unencumbered?

Only when you drink from the river of silence shall you indeed sing.

And when you have reached the mountain top, then you shall begin to climb.

And when the earth shall claim your limbs, then shall you truly dance.

ON FAREWELL

And now it was evening.

And Almitra the seeress said, Blessed be this day and this place and your spirit that has spoken.

And he answered, Was it I who spoke? Was I not also a listener?

Then he descended the steps of the Temple and all the people followed him. And he reached his ship and stood upon the deck.

And facing the people again, he raised his voice and said:

People of Orphalese, the wind bids me leave you.

Less hasty am I than the wind, yet I must go.

We wanderers, ever seeking the lonelier way, begin no day where we have ended another day; and no sunrise finds us where sunset left us. Even while the earth sleeps we travel.

We are the seeds of the tenacious plant, and it is in our ripeness and our fullness of heart that we are given to the wind and are scattered.

Brief were my days among you, and briefer still the words I have spoken.

But should my voice fade in your ears, and my love vanish in your memory, then I will come again,

And with a richer heart and lips more yielding to the spirit will I speak.

Yea, I shall return with the tide,

And though death may hide me, and the greater silence enfold me, yet again will I seek your understanding.

And not in vain will I seek.

If aught I have said is truth, that truth shall reveal itself in a clearer voice, and in words more kin to your thoughts.

I go with the wind, people of Orphalese, but not down into emptiness; And if this day is not a fulfilment of your needs and my love, then let it be a promise till another day.

Man's needs change, but not his love, nor his desire that his love should satisfy his needs.

Know therefore, that from the greater silence I shall return.

The mist that drifts away at dawn, leaving but dew in the fields, shall rise and gather into a cloud and then fall down in rain.

And not unlike the mist have I been.

In the stillness of the night I have walked in your streets, and my spirit has entered your houses,

And your heart-beats were in my heart, and your breath was upon my face, and I knew you all.

Ay, I knew your joy and your pain, and in your sleep your dreams were my dreams.

And oftentimes I was among you a lake among the mountains.

I mirrored the summits in you and the bending slopes, and even the passing flocks of your thoughts and your desires.

And to my silence came the laughter of your children in streams, and the longing of your youths in rivers.

And when they reached my depth the streams and the rivers ceased not yet to sing.

But sweeter still than laughter and greater than longing came to me.

It was the boundless in you;

The vast man in whom you are all but cells and sinews;

He in whose chant all your singing is but a soundless throbbing.

It is in the vast man that you are vast,

And in beholding him that I beheld you and loved you.

For what distances can love reach that are not in that vast sphere?

What visions, what expectations and what presumptions can outsoar that flight?

Like a giant oak tree covered with apple blossoms is the vast man in you. His might binds you to the earth, his fragrance lifts you into space, and in his durability you are deathless.

You have been told that, even like a chain, you are as weak as your weakest link.

This is but half the truth. You are also as strong as your strongest link.

To measure you by your smallest deed is to reckon the power of ocean by the frailty of its foam.

To judge you by your failures is to cast blame upon the seasons for their inconstancy.

Ay, you are like an ocean,

And though heavy-grounded ships await the tide upon your shores, yet, even like an ocean, you cannot hasten your tides.

And like the seasons you are also,

And though in your winter you deny your spring,

Yet spring, reposing within you, smiles in her drowsiness and is not offended. Think not I say these things in order that you may say the one to the other, "He praised us well. He saw but the good in us."

I only speak to you in words of that which you yourselves know in thought.

And what is word knowledge but a shadow of wordless knowledge?

Your thoughts and my words are waves from a sealed memory that keeps records of our yesterdays,

And of the ancient days when the earth knew not us nor herself,

And of nights when earth was up-wrought with confusion.

Wise men have come to you to give you of their wisdom. I came to take of your wisdom:

And behold I have found that which is greater than wisdom.

It is a flame spirit in you ever gathering more of itself,

While you, heedless of its expansion, bewail the withering of your days. It is life in quest of life in bodies that fear the grave.

There are no graves here.

These mountains and plains are a cradle and a stepping-stone.

Whenever you pass by the field where you have laid your ancestors look well thereupon, and you shall see yourselves and your children dancing hand in hand.

Verily you often make merry without knowing.

Others have come to you to whom for golden promises made unto your faith you have given but riches and power and glory.

Less than a promise have I given, and yet more generous have you been to me.

You have given me my deeper thirsting after life.

Surely there is no greater gift to a man than that which turns all his aims into parching lips and all life into a fountain.

And in this lies my honour and my reward,—

That whenever I come to the fountain to drink I find the living water itself thirsty;

And it drinks me while I drink it.

Some of you have deemed me proud and over-shy to receive gifts.

Too proud indeed am I to receive wages, but not gifts.

And though I have eaten berries among the hills when you would have had me sit at your board,

And slept in the portico of the temple when you would gladly have sheltered me,

Yet was it not your loving mindfulness of my days and my nights that made food sweet to my mouth and girdled my sleep with visions?

For this I bless you most:

You give much and know not that you give at all. Verily the kindness that gazes upon itself in a mirror turns to stone,

And a good deed that calls itself by tender names becomes the parent to a curse.

And some of you have called me aloof, and drunk with my own aloneness,

And you have said, "He holds council with the trees of the forest, but not with men.

He sits alone on hill-tops and looks down upon our city."

True it is that I have climbed the hills and walked in remote places.

How could I have seen you save from a great height or a great distance?

How can one be indeed near unless he be far?

And others among you called unto me, not in words, and they said,

"Stranger, stranger, lover of unreachable heights, why dwell you among the summits where eagles build their nests? Why seek you the unattainable?

What storms would you trap in your net,

And what vaporous birds do you hunt in the sky?

Come and be one of us.

Descend and appease your hunger with our bread and quench your thirst with our wine."

In the solitude of their souls they said these things;

But were their solitude deeper they would have known that I sought but the secret of your joy and your pain,

And I hunted only your larger selves that walk the sky.

But the hunter was also the hunted;

For many of my arrows left my bow only to seek my own breast.

And the flier was also the creeper;

For when my wings were spread in the sun their shadow upon the earth was a turtle.

And I the believer was also the doubter; For often have I put my finger in my own wound that I might have the greater belief in you and the greater knowledge of you.

And it is with this belief and this knowledge that I say,

You are not enclosed within your bodies, nor confined to houses or fields.

That which is you dwells above the mountain and roves with the wind.

It is not a thing that crawls into the sun for warmth or digs holes into darkness for safety,

But a thing free, a spirit that envelops the earth and moves in the ether.

If these be vague words, then seek not to clear them.

Vague and nebulous is the beginning of all things, but not their end,

And I fain would have you remember me as a beginning.

Life, and all that lives, is conceived in the mist and not in the crystal. And who knows but a crystal is mist in decay?

This would I have you remember in remembering me:

That which seems most feeble and bewildered in you is the strongest and most determined.

Is it not your breath that has erected and hardened the structure of your bones?

And is it not a dream which none of you remember having dreamt, that builded your city and fashioned all there is in it?

Could you but see the tides of that breath you would cease to see all else,

And if you could hear the whispering of the dream you would hear no other sound.

But you do not see, nor do you hear, and it is well.

The veil that clouds your eyes shall be lifted by the hands that wove it,

And the clay that fills your ears shall be pierced by those fingers that kneaded it. And you shall see.

And you shall hear.

Yet you shall not deplore having known blindness, nor regret having been deaf.

For in that day you shall know the hidden purposes in all things,

And you shall bless darkness as you would bless light.

After saying these things he looked about him, and he saw the pilot of his ship standing by the helm and gazing now at the full sails and now at the distance.

And he said:

Patient, over patient, is the captain of my ship.

The wind blows, and restless are the sails;

Even the rudder begs direction;

Yet quietly my captain awaits my silence.

And these my mariners, who have heard the choir of the greater sea, they too have heard me patiently. Now they shall wait no longer.

I am ready.

The stream has reached the sea, and once more the great mother holds her son against her breast.

Fare you well, people of Orphalese.

This day has ended.

It is closing upon us even as the water-lily upon its own tomorrow.

What was given us here we shall keep,

And if it suffices not, then again must we come together and together stretch our hands unto the giver.

Forget not that I shall come back to you.

A little while, and my longing shall gather dust and foam for another body.

A little while, a moment of rest upon the wind, and another woman shall bear me.

Farewell to you and the youth I have spent with you.

It was but yesterday we met in a dream. You have sung to me in my aloneness, and I of your longings have built a tower in the sky.

But now our sleep has fled and our dream is over, and it is no longer dawn.

The noontide is upon us and our half waking has turned to fuller day, and we must part.

If in the twilight of memory we should meet once more, we shall speak again together and you shall sing to me a deeper song.

And if our hands should meet in another dream we shall build another tower in the sky.

So saying he made a signal to the seamen, and straightway they weighed anchor and cast the ship loose from its moorings, and they moved eastward.

And a cry came from the people as from a single heart, and it rose into the dusk and was carried out over the sea like a great trumpeting.

Only Almitra was silent, gazing after the ship until it had vanished into the mist.

And when all the people were dispersed she still stood alone upon the sea-wall, remembering in her heart his saying,

The End